CREATIVE'S CLASSIC STORIES

This short story is taken out of an anthology and presented in its own volume where it stands a better chance of being read and remembered.

In one story, we might see a character survive extreme loneliness, danger, or sadness. Reading about such characters and events can be a powerful experience. And once we've read a good story, it can stay dormant in our memories for years and come to the surface later when we need its wisdom in facing our own danger, loneliness or sadness.

This short story is a well-told classic which has stood the test of time. It is included in Creative's Classic Stories Series and presented with all the dignity and richness a good classic story deserves.

THE ENEMY

THE ENEMY

PEARL S. BUCK

Creative Education, Inc.
Mankato, Minnesota

Published by Creative Education, Inc.
123 South Broad Street, Mankato, Minnesota 56001

Library of Congress Cataloging-in-Publication Data

Buck, Pearl, 1892-1973.
  The Enemy.

  Reprinted from Harper's Magazine by Pearl Buck.
  (Creative's classic short stories)
  I. Title. II. Series.
PS3503.U198E53 1986   813'.52   85-30005
ISBN 0-88682-059-6

To

the continuation of fine literature

for readers of all ages.

Dr. Sadao Hoki's house was built on a spot of the Japanese coast where as a little boy he had often played. The low square stone house was set upon rocks well above a narrow beach that was outlined with bent pines. As a boy Sadao had climbed the pines, supporting himself on his bare feet, as he had seen men do in the South Seas when they climbed for coconuts. His father had taken him often to the islands of those seas, and never had he failed to say to the little grave boy at his side, "Those islands yonder, they are the steppingstones to the future for Japan."

"Where shall we step from them?" Sadao had asked seriously.

"Who knows?" his father had answered. "Who can limit our future? It depends on what we make it."

Sadao had taken this into his mind as he did everything his father said, his father who never joked or played with him but who spent infinite pains upon him who was his only son. Sadao knew that his education was his father's chief concern. For this reason he had been sent at twenty-two to America to learn all that could be learned of surgery and medicine. He had come back at thirty, and before his father died he had seen Sadao become famous not only as a surgeon but as a scientist. Because he was now perfecting a discovery which would render wounds entirely clean he had not been sent abroad with the troops. Also, he knew, there was some slight danger that the old General might need an operation for a condition for which he was now being treated

medically, and for this possibility Sadao was being kept
in Japan.

Clouds were rising from the ocean now. The
unexpected warmth of the past few days had at night
drawn heavy fog from the old waves. Sadao watched
mists hide outlines of a little island near the shore and
then come creeping up the beach below the house,
wreathing around the pines. In a few minutes fog
would be wrapped about the house too. Then he
would go into the room where Hana, his wife, would
be waiting for him with the two children.

But at this moment the door opened and she
looked out, a dark blue woolen haori over her kimono.
She came to him affectionately and put her arm
through his as he stood, smiled and said nothing. He
had met Hana in America, but he had waited to fall in
love with her until he was sure she was Japanese. His

father would never have received her unless she had been pure in her race. He wondered often whom he would have married if he had not met Hana, and by what luck he had found her in the most casual way, by chance literally, at an American professor's house. The professor and his wife had been kind people anxious to do something for their few foreign students, and the students, though bored, had accepted this kindness. Sadao had often told Hana how nearly he had not gone to Professor Harley's house that night—the rooms were so small, the food so bad, the professor's wife so voluble. But he had gone and there he had found Hana, a new student, and had felt he would love her if it were at all possible.

Now he felt her hand on his arm and was aware of the pleasure it gave him, even though they had been married years enough to have the two children. For they had not married heedlessly in America. They had finished their work at school and had come home to Japan, and when his father had seen her the marriage had been arranged in the old Japanese way, although Sadao and Hana had talked everything over beforehand. They were perfectly happy. She laid her cheek against his arm.

It was at this moment that both of them saw something black come out of the mists. It was a man. He was flung up out of the ocean—flung, it seemed, to his feet by a breaker. He staggered a few steps, his body outlined against the mist, his arms above his head. Then the curled mists hid him again.

"Who is that?" Hana cried. She dropped Sadao's arm and they both leaned over the railing of the veranda. Now they saw him again. The man was on his hands and knees crawling. Then they saw him fall on his face and lie there.

"A fisherman perhaps," Sadao said, "washed from his boat." He ran quickly down the steps, and behind him Hana came, her wide sleeves flying. A mile or two away on either side there were fishing villages, but here was only the bare and lonely coast, dangerous with rocks. The surf beyond the beach was spiked with rocks. Somehow the man had managed to come through them—he must be badly torn.

They saw when they came toward him that indeed it was so. The sand on one side of him had already a stain of red soaking through.

"He is wounded," Sadao exclaimed. He made haste to the man, who lay motionless, his face in the sand. An old cap stuck to his head soaked with sea water. He was in wet rags of garments. Sadao stooped, Hana at his side, and turned the man's head. They saw the face.

"A white man!" Hana whispered.

Yes, it was a white man. The wet cap fell away and there was his wet yellow hair, long, as though for many weeks it had not been cut, and upon his young and tortured face was a rough yellow beard. He was unconscious and knew nothing that they did to him.

Now Sadao remembered the wound, and with his expert fingers he began to search for it. Blood flowed freshly at his touch. On the right side of his lower back Sadao saw that a gun wound had been reopened. The flesh was blackened with powder. Sometime, not many days ago, the man had been shot and had not been tended. It was bad chance that the rock had struck the wound.

"Oh, how he is bleeding!" Hana whispered again in a solemn voice. The mists screened them now

completely, and at this time of day no one came by.
The fishermen had gone home and even the chance
beachcombers would have considered the day at an
end.

"What shall we do with this man?" Sadao
muttered. But his trained hands seemed of their own
will to be doing what they could to stanch the fearful
bleeding. He packed the wound with the sea moss that
strewed the beach. The man moaned with pain in his
stupor but he did not awaken.

"The best thing that we could do would be to put
him back in the sea," Sadao said, answering himself.

Now that the bleeding was stopped for the moment
he stood up and dusted the sand from his hands.

"Yes, undoubtedly that would be best," Hana said
steadily. But she continued to stare down at the
motionless man.

"If we sheltered a white man in our house we should be arrested and if we turned him over as a prisoner, he would certainly die," Sadao said.

"The kindest thing would be to put him back into the sea," Hana said. But neither of them moved. They were staring with a curious repulsion upon the inert figure.

"What is he?" Hana whispered.

"There is something about him that looks American," Sadao said. He took up the battered cap. Yes, there, almost gone, was the faint lettering. "A sailor," he said, "from an American warship." He spelled it out: "U.S. Navy." The man was a prisoner of war!

"He has escaped," Hana cried softly, "and that is why he is wounded."

"In the back," Sadao agreed.

They hesitated, looking at each other. Then Hana said with resolution:

"Come, are we able to put him back into the sea?"

"If I am able, are you?" Sadao asked.

"No," Hana said. "But if you can do it alone..."

Sadao hesitated again. "The strange thing is," he said, "that if the man were whole I could turn him over to the police without difficulty. I care nothing for him. He is my enemy. All Americans are my enemy. And he is only a common fellow. You see how foolish his face is. But since he is wounded..."

"You also cannot throw him back to the sea," Hana said. "Then there is only one thing to do. We must carry him into the house."

"But the servants?" Sadao inquired.

"We must simply tell them that we intend to give him to the police—as indeed we must, Sadao. We must

think of the children and your position. It would
endanger all of us if we did not give this man over as a
prisoner of war."

"Certainly," Sadao agreed. "I would not think of
doing anything else.

Thus agreed, together they lifted the man. He was
very light, like a fowl that has been half starved for a
long time until it is only feathers and skeleton. So, his
arms hanging, they carried him up the steps and into
the side door of the house. This door opened into a
passage and down the passage they carried the man
toward an empty bedroom. It had been the bedroom
of Sadao's father and since his death it had not been
used. They laid the man on the deeply matted floor.
Everything here had been Japanese to please the old
man, who would never in his own home sit on a chair
or sleep in a foreign bed. Hana went to the wall

cupboards and slid back a door and took out a soft
quilt. She hesitated. The quilt was covered with
flowered silk and the lining was pure white silk.

"He is so dirty," she murmured in distress.

"Yes, he had better be washed," Sadao agreed. "If
you will fetch hot water I will wash him."

"I cannot bear for you to touch him," she said.
"We shall have to tell the servants he is here. I will tell
Yumi now. She can leave the children for a few
minutes and she can wash him."

Sadao considered a moment. "Let it be so," he
agreed. "You tell Yumi and I will tell the others."

But the utter pallor of the man's unconscious face
moved him first to stoop and feel his pulse. It was faint
but it was there. He put his hand against the man's
cold breast. The heart too was yet alive.

"He will die unless he is operated on," Sadao said,

considering. "The question is whether he will not die anyway."

Hana cried out in fear. "Don't try to save him! What if he should live?"

"What if he should die?" Sadao replied. He stood gazing down on the motionless man. This man must have extraordinary vitality or he would have been dead by now. But then he was very young—perhaps not yet twenty-five.

"You mean die from the operation?" Hana asked.

"Yes," Sadao said.

Hana considered this doubtfully, and when she did not answer Sadao turned away. "At any rate something must be done with him," he said, "and first he must be washed." He went quickly out of the room and Hana came behind him. She did not wish to be left alone with the white man. He was the first she had seen since she left America and now he seemed to have nothing to do with those whom she had known there. Here he was her enemy, a menace, living or dead.

She turned to the nursery and called, "Yumi!"

But the children heard her voice and she had to go in for a moment and smile at them and play with the baby boy, now nearly three months old.

Over the baby's soft black hair she motioned with her mouth, "Yumi—come with me!"

"I will put the baby to bed," Yumi replied. "He is ready."

She went with Yumi into the bedroom next to the nursery and stood with the boy in her arms while Yumi spread the sleeping quilts on the floor and laid the baby between them.

Then Hana led the way quickly and softly to the kitchen. The two servants were frightened at what their master had just told them. The old gardener who was also a house servant pulled the few hairs on his upper lip.

"The master ought not to heal the wound of this white man," he said bluntly to Hana. "The white man ought to die. First he was shot. Then the sea caught him and wounded him with her rocks. If the master heals what the gun did and what the sea did they will take revenge on us."

"I will tell him what you say," Hana replied courteously. But she herself was also frightened, although she was not superstitious as the old man was. Could it ever be well to help an enemy? Nevertheless she told Yumi to fetch the hot water and bring it to the room where the white man was.

She went ahead and slid back the partitions. Sadao was not yet there. Yumi, following, put down her wooden bucket. Then she went over to the white man. When she saw him her thick lips folded themselves into stubbornness. "I have never washed a white man," she said, "and I will not wash so dirty a one now."

Hana cried at her severely, "You will do what your master commands you!"

"My master ought not to command me to wash the enemy," Yumi said stubbornly.

There was so fierce a look of resistance upon Yumi's round dull face that Hana felt unreasonably afraid. After all, if the servants should report something that was not as it happened?

"Very well," she said with dignity. "You understand we only want to bring him to his senses so that we can turn him over as a prisoner?"

"I will have nothing to do with it," Yumi said. "I am a poor person and it is not my business."

"Then please," Hana said gently, "return to your own work."

At once Yumi left the room. But this left Hana with the white man alone. She might have been too afraid to stay had not her anger at Yumi's stubbornness now sustained her.

"Stupid Yumi," she muttered fiercely. "Is this anything but a man? And a wounded, helpless man!"

In the conviction of her own superiority she bent impulsively and untied the knotted rags that kept the white man covered. When she had his breast bare she dipped the small clean towel that Yumi had brought into the steaming hot water and washed his face carefully. The man's skin, though rough with exposure, was of a fine texture and must have been very blond when he was a child.

While she was thinking these thoughts, though not

really liking the man better now that he was no longer a child, she kept on washing him until his upper body was quite clean. But she dared not turn him over. Where was Sadao? Now her anger was ebbing and she was anxious again and she rose, wiping her hands on the wrung towel. Then lest the man be chilled she put the quilt over him.

"Sadao!" she called softly.

He had been about to come in when she called. His hand had been on the door and now he opened it. She saw that he had brought his surgeon's emergency bag and that he wore his surgeon's coat.

"You have decided to operate!" she cried.

"Yes," he said shortly. He turned his back to her and unfolded a sterilized towel upon the floor of the *takonoma* alcove, and put his instruments out upon it.

"Fetch towels," he said.

She went obediently, but how anxious now, to the linen shelves and took out the towels. There ought also to be old pieces of matting so that the blood would not ruin the fine floor covering. She went out to the back veranda where the gardener kept strips of matting with which to protect delicate shrubs on cold nights and took an armful of them.

But when she went back into the room she saw this was useless. The blood had already soaked through the packing in the man's wound and had ruined the mat under him.

"Oh, the mat!" she cried.

"Yes, it is ruined," Sadao replied, as though he did not care. "Help me to turn him," he commanded her.

She obeyed him without a word, and he began to wash the man's back carefully.

"Yumi would not wash him," she said.

"Did you wash him, then?" Sadao asked, not stopping for a moment his swift concise movements.

"Yes," she said.

He did not seem to hear her. But she was used to his absorption when he was at work. She wondered for a moment if it mattered to him what was the body upon which he worked so long as it was for the work he did so excellently.

"You will have to give the anesthetic if he needs it," he said.

"I?" she repeated blankly. "But never have I!"

"It is easy enough," he said impatiently.

He was taking out the packing now and the blood began to flow more quickly. He peered into the wound with the bright surgeon's light fastened on his forehead. "The bullet is still there," he said with cool interest. "Now I wonder how deep this rock wound is. If it is not too deep it may be that I can get the bullet. But the bleeding is not superficial. He has lost much blood."

At this moment Hana choked. He looked up and saw her face the color of sulphur.

"Don't faint," he said sharply. He did not put down his exploring instrument. "If I stop now the man will surely die." She clapped her hands to her mouth and leaped up and ran out of the room. Outside in the garden he heard her retching. But he went on with his work.

"It will be better for her to empty her stomach," he thought. He had forgotten that of course she had never seen an operation. But her distress and his inability to go to her at once made him impatient and irritable with this man who lay like dead under his knife.

"This man," he thought, "there is no reason under heaven why he should live."

Unconsciously this thought made him ruthless and he proceeded swiftly. In his dream the man moaned, but Sadao paid no heed except to mutter at him.

"Groan," he muttered, "groan if you like. I am not doing this for my own pleasure. In fact, I do not know why I am doing it."

The door opened and there was Hana again. She had not stopped even to smooth back her hair.

"Where is the anesthetic?" she asked in a clear voice.

Sadao motioned with his chin. "It is as well that you came back," he said. "This fellow is beginning to stir."

She had the bottle and some cotton in her hand.

"But how shall I do it?" she asked.

"Simply saturate the cotton and hold it near his nostrils," Sadao replied without delaying for one moment the intricate detail of his work. "When he breathes badly move it away a little."

She crouched close to the sleeping face of the young American. It was a piteously thin face, she thought, and the lips were twisted. The man was suffering whether he knew it or not. Watching him, she wondered if the stories they heard sometimes of the sufferings of prisoners were true. They came like flickers of rumor, told by word of mouth and always contradicted. In the newspapers the reports were always that wherever the Japanese armies went the people received them gladly, with cries of joy at their liberation. But sometimes she remembered such men as General Takima, who at home beat his wife cruelly, though no one mentioned it now that he had fought so victorious a battle in Manchuria. If a man like that could be so cruel to a woman in his power, would he not be cruel to one like this for instance?

She hoped anxiously that this young man had not been tortured. It was at this moment that she observed deep red scars on his neck, just under the ear. "Those scars," she murmured, lifting her eyes to Sadao.

But he did not answer. At this moment he felt the tip of his instrument strike against something hard, dangerously near the kidney. All thought left him. He felt only the purest pleasure. He probed with his fingers, delicately, familiar with every atom of this human body. His old American professor of anatomy had seen to that knowledge. "Ignorance of the human body is the surgeon's cardinal sin, sirs!" he had thundered at his classes year after year. "To operate without as complete knowledge of the body as if you had made it—anything less than that is murder."

"It is not quite at the kidney, my friend," Sadao murmured. It was his habit to murmur to the patient when he forgot himself in an operation. "My friend," he always called his patients and so now he did, forgetting that this was his enemy.

Then quickly, with the cleanest and most precise of incisions, the bullet was out. The man quivered but he was still unconscious. Nevertheless he muttered a few English words.

"Guts," he muttered, choking. "They got...my guts.."

"Sadao!" Hana cried sharply.

"Hush," Sadao said.

The man sank again into silence so profound that Sadao took up his wrist, hating the touch of it. Yes, there was still a pulse so faint, so feeble, but enough, if he wanted the man to live, to give hope.

"But certainly I do not want this man to live," he thought.

"No more anesthetic," he told Hana.

He turned as swiftly as though he had never paused and from his medicines he chose a small vial and from it filled a hypodermic and thrust it into the patient's left arm. Then, putting down the needle, he took the man's wrist again. The pulse under his fingers fluttered once or twice and then grew stronger.

"This man will live in spite of all," he said to Hana and sighed.

The young man woke, so weak, his blue eyes so terrified when he perceived where he was, that Hana felt compelled to apology. She served him herself, for none of the servants would enter the room.

When she came in the first time she saw him

summon his small strength to be prepared for some
fearful thing.

"Don't be afraid," she begged him softly.

"How come...you speak English?" he gasped.

"I was a long time in America," she replied.

She saw that he wanted to reply to that but he
could not, and so she knelt and fed him gently from
the porcelain spoon. He ate unwillingly, but still he
ate.

Now you will soon be strong," she said, not liking
him and yet moved to comfort him.

He did not answer.

When Sadao came in the third day after the
operation he found the young man sitting up, his face
bloodless with the effort.

"Lie down," Sadao cried. "Do you want to die?"

He forced the man down gently and strongly and

examined the wound. "You may kill yourself if you do this sort of thing," he scolded.

"What are you going to do with me?" the boy muttered. He looked just now barely seventeen. "Are you going to hand me over?"

For a moment Sadao did not answer. He finished his examination and then pulled the silk quilt over the man.

"I do not know myself what I shall do with you," he said. "I ought of course to give you to the police. You are a prisoner of war—no, do not tell me anything." He put up his hand as he saw the young man about to speak. "Do not even tell me your name unless I ask it."

They looked at each other for a moment, and then the young man closed his eyes and turned his face to the wall.

"Okay," he whispered, his mouth a bitter line.

Outside the door Hana was waiting for Sadao. He saw at once that she was in trouble.

"Sadao, Yumi tells me the servants feel they cannot stay if we hide this man here any more," she said. "She tells me that they are saying that you and I were so long in America that we have forgotten to think of our own country first. They think we like Americans."

"It is not true," Sadao said harshly, "Americans are our enemies. But I have been trained not to let a man die if I can help it."

"The servants cannot understand that," she said anxiously.

"No," he agreed.

Neither seemed able to say more, and somehow the household dragged on. The servants grew daily more watchful. Their courtesy was as careful as ever, but

37

their eyes were cold upon the pair to whom they were hired.

"It is clear what our master ought to do," the old gardener said one morning. He had worked with flowers all his life, and had been a specialist too in moss. For Sadao's father he had made one of the finest moss gardens in Japan, sweeping the bright green carpet constantly so that not a leaf or a pine needle marred the velvet of its surface. "My old master's son knows very well what he ought to do," he now said, pinching a bud from a bush as he spoke. "When the man was so near death why did he not let him bleed?"

"That young master is so proud of his skill to save life that he saves any life," the cook said contemptuously. She split a fowl's neck skillfully and held the fluttering bird and let its blood flow into the roots of a wistaria vine. Blood is the best of fertilizers, and the old gardener would not let her waste a drop of it.

"It is the children of whom we must think," Yumi said sadly. "What will be their fate if their father is condemned as a traitor?"

They did not try to hide what they said from the ears of Hana as she stood arranging the day's flowers in the veranda near by, and she knew they spoke on purpose that she might hear. That they were right she knew too in most of her being. But there was another part of her which she herself could not understand. It was not sentimental liking of the prisoner. She had come to think of him as a prisoner. She had not liked him even yesterday when he had said in his impulsive way, "Anyway, let me tell you that my name is Tom." She had only bowed her little distant bow. She saw hurt in his eyes but she did not wish to assuage it.

Indeed, he was a great trouble in this house.

As for Sadao, every day he examined the wound carefully. The last stitches had been pulled out this morning, and the young man would in a fortnight be nearly as well as ever. Sadao went back to his office and carefully typed a letter to the chief of police reporting the whole matter. "On the twenty-first day of February an escaped prisoner was washed up on the shore in front of my house." So far he typed and then he opened a secret drawer of his desk and put the unfinished report into it.

On the seventh day after that two things happened. In the morning the servants left together, their belongings tied in large square cotton kerchiefs. When Hana got up in the morning nothing was done, the house not cleaned and the food not prepared, and she knew what it meant. She was dismayed and even terrified, but her pride as a mistress would not allow her to show it. Instead she inclined her head gracefully when they appeared before her in the kitchen, and she paid them off and thanked them for all that they had done for her. They were crying, but she did not cry. The cook and the gardener had served Sadao since he was a little boy in his father's house, and Yumi cried because of the children. She was so grieving that after she had gone she ran back to Hana.

"If the baby misses me too much tonight send for me. I am going to my own house and you know where it is."

"Thank you," Hana said, smiling. But she told herself she would not send for Yumi however the baby cried.

She made the breakfast and Sadao helped with the children. Neither of them spoke of the servants beyond

the fact that they were gone. But after Hana had taken
morning food to the prisoner she came back to Sadao.

"Why is it we cannot see clearly what we ought to
do?" she asked him. "Even the servants see more
clearly than we do. Why are we different from other
Japanese?"

Sadao did not answer. But a little later he went
into the room where the prisoner was and said
brusquely, "Today you may get up on your feet. I
want you to stay up only five minutes at a time.
Tomorrow you may try it twice as long. It would be
well that you get back your strength as quickly as
possible."

He saw the flicker of terror on the young face that
was still very pale.

"Okay," the boy murmured. Evidently he was
determined to say more. "I feel I ought to thank you,

Doctor, for having saved my life."

"Don't thank me too early," Sadao said coldly. He saw the flicker of terror again in the boy's eyes—terror as unmistakable as an animal's. The scars on his neck were crimson for a moment. Those scars! What were they? Sadao did not ask.

In the afternoon the second thing happened. Hana, working hard on unaccustomed labor, saw a messenger come to the door in official uniform. Her hands went weak and she could not draw her breath. The servants must have told already. She ran to Sadao, gasping, unable to utter a word. But by then the messenger had simply followed her through the garden and there he stood. She pointed at him helplessly.

Sadao looked up from his book. He was in his office, the outer partition of which was thrown open to the garden for the southern sunshine.

"What is it?" he asked the messenger, and then he rose, seeing the man's uniform.

"You are to come to the palace," the man said, "the old General is in pain again."

"Oh," Hana breathed, "is that all?"

"All!" the messenger exclaimed. "Is it not enough?"

"Indeed it is," she replied. "I am very sorry."

When Sadao came to say good-by she was in the kitchen, but doing nothing. The children were asleep and she sat merely resting for a moment, more exhausted from her fright than from work.

"I thought they had come to arrest you," she said.

He gazed down into her anxious eyes. "I must get rid of this man for your sake," he said in distress. "Somehow I must get rid of him."

"Of course," the General said weakly, "I understand fully. But that is because I once took a degree in

Princeton. So few Japanese have."

"I care nothing for the man, Excellency," Sadao said, "but having operated on him with such success..."

"Yes, yes," the General said. "It only makes me feel you more indispensable to me. Evidently you can save anyone—you are so skilled. You say you think I can stand one more such attack as I have had today?"

"Not more than one," Sadao said.

"Then certainly I can allow nothing to happen to you," the General said with anxiety. His long, pale, Japanese face became expressionless, which meant that he was in deep thought. "You cannot be arrested," the General said, closing his eyes. "Suppose you were condemned to death and the next day I had to have my operation?"

"There are other surgeons, Excellency," Sadao

suggested.

"None I trust," the General replied. "The best ones have been trained by Germans and would consider the operation successful even if I died. I do not care for their point of view." He sighed. "It seems a pity that we cannot better combine the German ruthlessness with the American sentimentality. Then you could turn your prisoner over to execution and yet I could be sure you would not murder me while I was unconscious." The General laughed. He had an unusual sense of humor. "As a Japanese, could you not combine these two foreign elements?" he asked.

Sadao smiled. "I am not quite sure," he said, "but for your sake I would be willing to try, Excellency."

The General shook his head. "I had rather not be the test case," he said. He felt suddenly weak and overwhelmed with the cares of his life as an official in times such as these when repeated victory brought great responsibilities all over the south Pacific. "It is very unfortunate that this man should have washed up on your doorstep," he said irritably.

"I feel it so myself," Sadao said gently.

"It would be best if he could be quietly killed," the General said. "Not by you, but by someone who does not know him. I have my own private assassins. Suppose I send two of them to your house tonight—or better, any night. You need know nothing about it. It is now warm—what would be more natural than that you should leave the outer partition of the white man's room open to the garden while he sleeps?"

"Certainly it would be very natural," Sadao agreed. "In fact, it is so left open every night."

"Good," the General said, yawning. "They are very capable assassins—they make no noise and they know the trick of inward bleeding. If you like I can even have them remove the body."

Sadao considered. "That perhaps would be best, Excellency," he agreed, thinking of Hana.

He left the General's presence then and went home, thinking over the plan. In this way the whole thing would be taken out of his hands. He would tell Hana nothing, since she would be timid at the idea of assassins in the house, and yet certainly such persons were essential in an absolute state such as Japan was. How else could rulers deal with those who opposed them?

He refused to allow anything but reason to be the atmosphere of his mind as he went into the room where the American was in bed. But as he opened the door, to his surprise he found the young man out of bed, and preparing to go into the garden.

"What is this!" he exclaimed. "Who gave you permission to leave your room?"

"I'm not used to waiting for permission," Tom said gaily. "Gosh, I feel pretty good again! But will the muscles on this side always feel stiff?"

"Is it so?" Sadao inquired, surprised. He forgot all else. "Now I thought I had provided against that," he murmured. He lifted the edge of the man's shirt and gazed at the healing scar. "Massage may do it," he said, "if exercise does not."

"It won't bother me much," the young man said. His young face was gaunt under the stubbly blond beard. "Say, Doctor, I've got something I want to say to you. If I hadn't met a Jap like you—well, I wouldn't be alive today. I know that."

Sadao bowed but he could not speak.

"Sure, I know that," Tom went on warmly. His big

thin hands, gripping a chair, were white at the knuckles. "I guess if all the Japs were like you there wouldn't have been a war."

"Perhaps," Sadao said with difficulty. "And now I think you had better go back to bed."

He helped the boy back into bed and then bowed. "Good night," he said.

Sadao slept badly that night. Time and time again he woke, thinking he heard the rustling of footsteps, the sound of a twig broken or a stone displaced in the garden—a noise such as men might make who carried a burden.

The next morning he made the excuse to go first into the guest room. If the American were gone he then could simply tell Hana that so the General had directed. But when he opened the door he saw at once that it was not last night. There on the pillow was the

shaggy blond head. He could hear the peaceful
breathing of sleep and he closed the door again quietly.

"He is asleep," he told Hana. "He is almost well to
sleep like that."

"What shall we do with him?" Hana whispered her
old refrain.

Sadao shook his head. "I must decide in a day or
two," he promised.

But certainly, he thought, the second night must be
the night. There rose a wind that night, and he
listened to the sounds of bending boughs and whistling
partitions.

Hana woke too. "Ought we not to go and close
the sick man's partition?" she asked.

"No," Sadao said. "He is able now to do it for
himself."

But the next morning the American was still there.

Then the third night of course must be the night.
The wind changed to quiet rain and the garden was
full of the sound of dripping eaves and running springs.
Sadao slept a little better, but he woke at the sound of
a crash and leaped to his feet.

"What was that?" Hana cried. The baby woke at
her voice and began to wail. "I must go and see."

But he held her and would not let her move.

"Sadao," she cried, "what is the matter with you?"

"Don't go," he muttered, "don't go!"

His terror infected her and she stood breathless,
waiting. There was only silence. Together they crept
back into the bed, the baby between them.

Yet when he opened the door of the guest room in
the morning there was the young man. He was very
gay and had already washed and was now on his feet.
He had asked for a razor yesterday and had shaved

himself, and today there was a faint color in his cheeks.

"I am well," he said joyously.

Sadao drew his kimono round his weary body. He could not, he decided suddenly, go through another night. It was not that he cared for this young man's life. No, simply it was not worth the strain.

"You are well," Sadao agreed. He lowered his voice. "You are so well that I think if I put my boat on the shore tonight, with food and extra clothing in it, you might be able to row to that little island not far from the coast. It is so near the coast that it has not been worth fortifying. Nobody lives on it because in storm it is submerged. But this is not the season of storm. You could live there until you saw a Korean fishing boat pass by. They pass quite near the island because the water is many fathoms deep there."

The young man stared at him, slowly

comprehending. "Do I have to?" he asked.

"I think so," Sadao said gently. "You
understand—it is not hidden that you are here."

The young man nodded in perfect comprehension.
"Okay," he said simply.

Sadao did not see him again until evening. As
soon as it was dark he had dragged the stout boat
down to the shore and in it he put food and bottled
water that he had bought secretly during the day, as
well as two quilts he had bought at a pawnshop. The
boat he tied to a post in the water, for the tide was
high. There was no moon and he worked without a
flashlight.

When he came to the house he entered as though
he were just back from his work, and so Hana knew
nothing. "Yumi was here today," she said as she served
his supper. Though she was so modern, still she did

not eat with him. "Yumi cried over the baby," she went on with a sigh. "She misses him so."

"The servants will come back as soon as the foreigner is gone," Sadao said.

He went into the guest room that night before he went to bed and himself checked carefully the American's temperature, the state of the wound, and his heart and pulse. The pulse was irregular, but that was perhaps because of excitement. The young man's pale lips were pressed together and his eyes burned. Only the scars on his neck were red.

"I realize you are saving my life again," he told Sadao.

"Not at all," Sadao said. "It is only inconvenient to have you here any longer."

He had hesitated a good deal about giving the man a flashlight. But he had decided to give it to him after all. It was a small one, his own, which he used at night when he was called.

"If your food runs out before you catch a boat," he said, "signal me two flashes at the same instant the sun drops over the horizon. Do not signal in darkness, for it will be seen. If you are all right but still there, signal me once. You will find fish easy to catch but you must eat them raw. A fire would be seen."

"Okay," the young man breathed.

He was dressed now in the Japanese clothes which Sadao had given him, and at the last moment Sadao wrapped a black cloth about his blond head.

"Now," Sadao said.

The young American without a word shook Sadao's hand warmly and then walked quite well across the floor and down the step into the darkness of the garden. Once—twice—Sadao saw his light flash to find his way. But that would not be suspected. He waited until from the shore there was one more flash. Then he closed the partition. That night he slept.

"You say the man escaped?" the General asked faintly. He had been operated upon a week before, an emergency operation to which Sadao had been called in the night. For twelve hours Sadao had not been sure the General would live. The gall bladder was much involved. Then the old man had begun to breathe deeply again and to demand food. Sadao had not been able to ask about the assassins. So far as he knew they had never come. The servants had returned and Yumi had cleaned the guest room thoroughly and had burned sulphur in it to get the white man's smell out of it. Nobody said anything. Only the gardener was cross because he had got behind with his chrysanthemums.

But after a week Sadao felt the General was well

enough to be spoken to about the prisoner.

"Yes, Excellency, he escaped," Sadao now said. He coughed, signifying that he had not said all he might have said but was unwilling to disturb the General further. But the old man opened his eyes suddenly.

"That prisoner," he said with some energy, "did I not promise you I would kill him for you?"

"You did, Excellency," Sadao said.

"Well, well!" the old man said in a tone of amazement, "so I did! But you see, I was suffering a good deal. The truth is, I thought of nothing but myself. In short, I forgot my promise to you."

"I wondered, Your Excellency," Sadao murmured.

"It was certainly very careless of me," the General said. "But you understand it was not lack of patriotism or dereliction of duty." He looked anxiously at his doctor. "If the matter should come out you would understand that, wouldn't you?"

"Certainly, Your Excellency," Sadao said. He suddenly comprehended that the General was in the palm of his hand and that as a consequence he himself was perfectly safe. "I can swear to your loyalty, Excellency," he said to the old General, "and to your zeal against the enemy."

"You are a good man," the General murmured, and closed his eyes. "You will be rewarded."

But Sadao, searching the spot of black in the twilighted sea that night, had his reward. There was no prick of light in the dusk. No one was on the island. His prisoner was gone—safe, doubtless, for he had warned him to wait only for a Korean fishing boat.

He stood for a moment on the veranda, gazing out to the sea from whence the young man had come that other night. And into his mind, although without

reason, there came other white faces he had known—
the professor at whose house he had met Hana, a dull
man, and his wife had been a silly, talkative woman, in
spite of her wish to be kind. He remembered his old
teacher of anatomy, who had been so insistent on
mercy with the knife, and then he remembered the face
of his fat and slatternly landlady. He had had great
difficulty in finding a place to live in America because
he was a Japanese. The Americans were full of
prejudice and it had been bitter to live in it, knowing
himself their superior. How he had despised the
ignorant and dirty old woman who had at last
consented to house him in her miserable home! He
had once tried to be grateful to her because she had in
his last year nursed him through influenza, but it was
difficult, for she was no less repulsive to him in her

kindness. But then, white people were repulsive of course. It was a relief to be openly at war with them at last. Now he remembered the youthful, haggard face of his prisoner—white and repulsive.

"Strange," he thought, "I wonder why I could not kill him?"

Pearl S. Buck (1892-1973)

Pearl Buck said that she was as much Chinese as she was American. Born in West Virginia, her missionary parents took her to China a few months later.

Pearl grew up living right among the Chinese. Rather than live in a missionary compound, her parents chose a house among the native people, in a small city on the Yangtze River. Each day, Pearl's mother taught her school lessons in English, and in the afternoons her Chinese tutor came. When she was eighteen, she went to the United States to attend Randolph-Macon Woman's College in Virginia.

After graduating from college, she returned to China. Three years later she married John Lossing Buck, an American agricultural specialist. For the next five years she and her husband lived in a farming village in northern China. Pearl grew to love and admire the Chinese peasants and wanted to write about them. But she didn't have enough confidence yet to do it.

Then Pearl and her husband moved to Nanking, where they both taught at the University. There was much unrest in China at that time. In 1927 revolutionary armies invaded Nanking, and Pearl and her family had to flee for their lives.

Pearl's personal life created problems for her also. It was difficult for her to raise her mentally retarded daughter while she was trying to launch a writing career. Pearl soon found a way, however, to borrow some money and send her daughter to a special school for two years. This gave Pearl time to write. In a short time, her novel *The Good Earth* was published, and it brought her the Pulitzer Prize in 1932.

In 1934 she returned to the United States to live. She continued to write a steady stream of fiction, and won the Nobel Prize for Literature in 1938. She founded the East and West Association for the purpose of increasing understanding among the peoples of the world. Pearl adopted nine children of different nationalities and founded two agencies for the aid and adoption of Asian-American children. Her concern was always for children, "not because of a maternal instinct," she said, "for you know I am not a very maternal woman, but because children are the future."

DATE DUE			
Dec. 02			
JUN 0			
FEB 0 9 1994			
MAY 2 6 1996		WITHDRAWN	

WITHDRAWN

Buck, Pearl S.
(Pearl
Sydenstricker)

The enemy.